The author, Sally Grindley lives in Cooper's Hill,
Gloucestershire with her three young sons, and two cats.
She has a degree in French literature from Sussex University
and enjoys squash, tennis, knitting, reading and collecting
handmade wooden toys, and Noah's Ark books and toys.

The artist, Siobhan Dodds is a talented and successful young
illustrator. She graduated from Brighton College of Art and
lives and works in Brighton, Sussex.

Text copyright © Sally Grindley 1988
Illustrations copyright © Siobhan Dodds 1988

First published in Great Britain in 1988
by Simon & Schuster Ltd
Reprinted in 1991, 1993 and 1994

Reprinted in 1997 and 1998
by Macdonald Young Books
an imprint of Wayland Publishers Ltd
61 Western Road
Hove
BN3 1JD

Printed in Hong Kong by Wing King Tong Co Ltd

British Library Cataloguing in Publication available

ISBN: 0 7500 0881 4

WAKE UP, DAD!

Sally Grindley

Illustrated by Siobhan Dodds

MACDONALD YOUNG BOOKS

"Dad . . . Are you asleep, Dad?"

"Are you asleep, Dad?"

"It's morning, Dad. Look, it's light outside. I've been awake for ages and ages. So has Teddy."

"Wake up, Dad."

"I can tell you what time it is if you want me to. The big hand is pointing to seven and the little hand is pointing to six."

"Wake up, Dad."

"Will you mend my truck for me, Dad?
Look, the wheel's come off and it won't
roll. The bell's gone funny too, listen."

"Do you know what Johnny did yesterday? He pulled my hair like this, really hard, and he wouldn't say sorry. He should say sorry shouldn't he, Dad? I don't like him anymore."

"Can we go to the zoo today, Dad? You said we could go soon. I want to see the gorillas. They're my favourite. They bang on their chests like this and make a noise like this – AAH-OOOO-AAAH!"

"Wake up, Dad."

"Dad, there's a big spider on the floor.
It's right by your shoes. Do spiders go
into shoes? They could build their nests
in them couldn't they, Dad?"

"Watch this Dad, I can do cartwheels."

"I can do somersaults too. Backward ones
and forward ones."

"I think Yum Yum wants to come in,
Dad. She must want her breakfast. Shall
I let her in?
Here she is, Dad. She's come to say
good morning, haven't you Yum Yum?"

"She caught a mouse yesterday, Dad, but when she tried to get through the cat-flap she dropped it and it ran away."

"Wake up, Dad."

"Shall I go and get my recorder, Dad? I can nearly play a tune on it."

NO!

"Dad, I'm cold, Dad. Can I get into bed with you?"

"It's lovely and warm in here, isn't it?
Why don't we all go back to sleep?"

"Miaow!"